Whiskey Bravo Gets His Wings

written by
Ebony Sutton

illustrated by
Kathy Kerber

KT-162-088

AuthorHouse™ UK Ltd.
500 Avebury Boulevard
Central Milton Keynes, MK9 2BE
www.authorhouse.co.uk
Phone: 08001974150

©2008 Ebony Sutton. All rights reserved.

No part of this book may be reproduced, stored in a retrieval system, or transmitted by any means without the written permission of the author.

First published by AuthorHouse 6/26/2008

ISBN: 978-1-4343-5837-0 (sc)

Printed in the United States of America
Bloomington, Indiana

This book is printed on acid-free paper.

authorHOUSE®

Foreword

It gave me great pleasure when asked, to provide the foreword for this little book for young people. Having experienced the world of helicopter search and rescue (SAR) as a pilot for many years, it always surprised me that no one had grasped the idea of a rescue helicopter in book form, which mirrored one in real life. Coastguard Whiskey Bravo is a real helicopter that can be seen flying around the skies, used every day to rescue and assist people in real life and featured regularly on the BBC series 'Seaside Rescue'.

Now at last, we have the adventures of Rescue Whiskey Bravo. Having flown the real Whiskey Bravo myself on many occasions, this book is a fitting tribute to the wonderful contribution that this helicopter and the people within the world of SAR have made.

Captain Mike Roughton

At the edge of the cold, greyish blue sea sits the Base, unlike its name, which is very ordinary; the Base is a very special place.

Here at the Base, lives Oscar Charlie and all his friends. Oscar Charlie is the chief helicopter at the Search and Rescue Base and has been the chief helicopter for a very long time. Oscar Charlie has made lots and lots of rescues and has bravely rescued stranded yachts, divers, and walkers who have fallen down the cliffs. He has also rescued children that have been swept out to sea whilst playing on their lilos, and given them back safely to their mums and dads.

Oscar Charlie lives at the Base with Avcat the bowser who supplies all the fuel to keep Oscar Charlie flying. Other friends of Oscar Charlie's are the beautiful Felicity forklift, Trevor the tractor and the very serious Airport Manager, who looks after the whole Base.

One November day, the Airport Manager went to the hanger to speak to Oscar Charlie. "You have a very important day tomorrow, you have to go to Aberdoon to pick up all the Top Brass," said the Airport Manager.

"The Top Brass", said Oscar Charlie. "Who are they"?

"Well, Oscar Charlie", said the Airport Manager. "The Top Brass are very important people that make all kinds of important decisions"

The next morning, it was a dull and rainy day, there were big black clouds hanging over the Base. Oscar Charlie looked up at the sky and sighed. He was out on the runway taking on fuel from Avcat the bowser ready for his long journey to Aberdoon. "I don't much like the look of those clouds Avcat, I think this may be a bumpy ride." "Oh dear, oh dear", thought Oscar Charlie. "Cheer up, it's not like you to be sad about a journey" said Avcat.

Soon Oscar Charlie was airborne and circling round the Base whilst his friends below waved him goodbye and wished him a safe journey. As Oscar Charlie flew further north the clouds became blacker, it started to rain and it got heavier and heavier. The wind blew harder so Oscar Charlie pointed his nose into the wind, screwed up his eyes and flew harder.

By the time Oscar Charlie landed at Aberdoon, he was very tired and rain was dripping from his shiny rotor blades. He settled down inside the hanger next to a little helicopter called Whiskey Bravo. Whiskey Bravo was training to be a search and rescue helicopter and he was so excited when he saw Oscar Charlie, he had heard so much about him. Whiskey Bravo wanted to be brave just like him. "Please can you tell me some of your adventures", whispered Whiskey Bravo to Oscar Charlie. "Oh all right," smiled Oscar Charlie. Remembering when he was just like Whiskey Bravo, young and eager. "Just one story and then we must both get some sleep".

The next morning, when the hanger doors were open, both Whiskey Bravo and Oscar Charlie looked up at the black angry sky. Oscar Charlie was refuelled, all the Top Brass were aboard and he stood on the runway ready for take off. Whiskey Bravo stood to the right side of the runway watching on as Oscar Charlie was cleared for takeoff and flew into the sky. He hovered over Whiskey Bravo and then flew towards the biggest blackest clouds.

Soon, it was 'raining cats and dogs', the wind blew very hard, the thunder rolled and the lightening flashed across the sky. Suddenly, Oscar Charlie was struck by lightening, which made him shudder. Oscar Charlie was in real trouble! The lightening had damaged his instruments that helped him find his way and he had to send out a mayday call to Aberdoon for help.

Aberdoon received the mayday call. "What shall we do, we don't have anyone to send to help!" "Yes you do," piped up, Whiskey Bravo. "You can send me, I can do it". As quick as a flash Whiskey Bravo was fuelled, made ready and was standing on the runway. "Good luck Whiskey Bravo". "Take care Whiskey Bravo" came the voices from below as the little helicopter took off.

Whiskey Bravo flew as hard as he could through the black clouds, he dodged the lightening and tried to forget about the loud crashing thunder that made him shudder. "You can do it," he told himself. On and on he flew, until in the distance he saw Oscar Charlie zig zagging slowly through the sky. Soon Whiskey Bravo had caught up with Oscar Charlie. "Follow me Oscar Charlie, I will show you the way", Whiskey Bravo said. With a weak smile, Oscar Charlie followed behind Whiskey Bravo. He was so glad to see the little helicopter.

Soon Whiskey Bravo and Oscar Charlie were landing safe and sound at the Base. The Airport Manager and everyone were crowded around the runway to see them land. That night when both helicopters where safely tucked up in the hanger, Oscar Charlie said, "Thank you Whiskey Bravo, you were a very brave little helicopter, you deserve to get your search and rescue wings". The next day everyone was out on the runway, everyone that is except Whiskey Bravo, he had overslept! "Come on Whiskey Bravo, we are all waiting for you", said Trevor the tractor.

Whiskey Bravo sheepishly came out of the hanger onto the runway, his little face pink with embarrassment. Suddenly, a band started to play Whiskey Bravo looked around him wide eyed, there were the Top Brass, Oscar Charlie, the Airport Manager and a huge crowd of others. "Whiskey Bravo, you have been very brave, you have rescued Oscar Charlie and I am proud to give you your wings". "Well done Rescue Whiskey Bravo, you are now a real search and rescue helicopter, and you can now stay at the Base and take the place of Oscar Charlie, who is going to come back with us to Aberdoon", said the Top Brass.

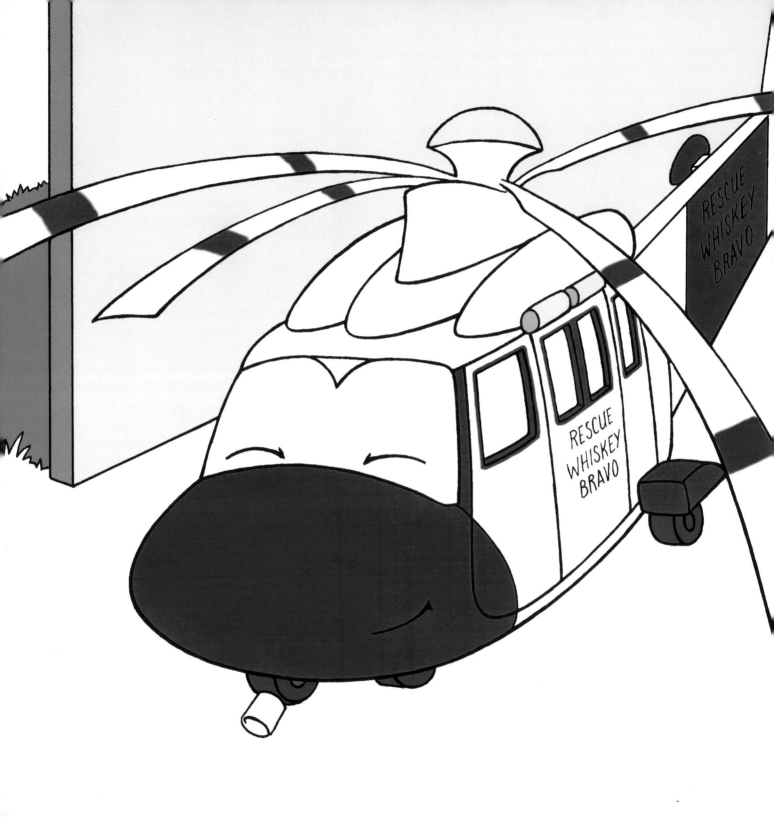

That night, Rescue Whiskey Bravo, settled down in his new hanger, he looked through the darkness at his new friends and smiled to himself. He was very happy and very excited. "Hurry up morning", he said to himself. "Hurry up!"

LaVergne, TN USA
18 February 2010
1704LVUK00003B

9 781434 358370